Here Comes
SANDY CLAUS
THE LAUNCH OF CHRISTMAS EVE

By Amy Leisner
Illustrated by Stephanie Dillon

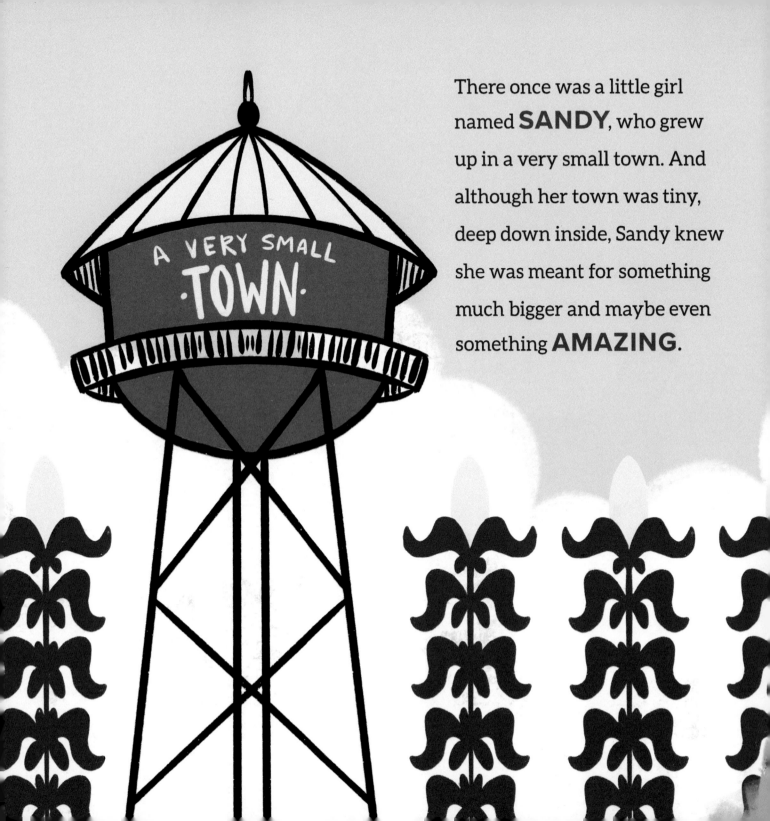

There once was a little girl named **SANDY**, who grew up in a very small town. And although her town was tiny, deep down inside, Sandy knew she was meant for something much bigger and maybe even something **AMAZING**.

She worked hard in school, made many friends, and loved to write, paint, and dance. Sandy liked being the leader, because then she could help her friends when they needed it.

Once she was old enough, Sandy left her small town for the big city to learn all about business so that she could start one of her own.

She was an **ENTREPRENEUR**.

That's a fancy way to say that she was the boss. Entrepreneurs get to come up with lots of fun ideas and turn them into businesses.

One day, she was out shopping at a market close to her house and met a nice young man who made **TOYS**.

"Those are some very nice toys you're making. I love the cars," Sandy said.

"Thank you very much. The cars are my favorite to make," Nick said.

"My name is Sandy. What's yours?"

"NICK."

They continued talking and got along really well.

Sandy and Nick soon spent all of their time together, talking, playing, and they fell deeply in **LOVE**.

They decided to get married and promised to always be **EQUAL PARTNERS**.

She supported him, and he supported her, and everything was **FAIR**.

One day, Nick suggested that they move to the **NORTH POLE!**

"I'm tired of the hot summers and would like
more space for building all of my toys."

Since Sandy's business was run on the internet, she could live anywhere, and because she knew how much it meant to her husband, she was happy to pack up and make the move.

"LET'S DO IT," she said.

At the North Pole, they had all this extra space, and Nick began making so many more toys of all different kinds. He made...

TRUCKS Musical instruments

Dolls **PUZZLES**

Animals Cars

BUILDING BLOCKS

and so much more!

And with all these toys piling up around them, this gave Sandy a **BIG IDEA**.

Sandy told Nick, "Wouldn't it be nice for every child in the whole wide world to get one of your toys? Christmas is a nice time for giving gifts. You should deliver the toys to each home on **CHRISTMAS EVE** so that each child wakes up to a new toy on Christmas Day."

"Well that would be very nice, but I can't make that many toys all by myself," said Nick.

"Of course not.

WE'LL OUTSOURCE,"

Sandy replied.

Sandy posted an advertisement the next day and got the most lovely response from a group of **ELVES** looking for work, who also happened to come from a long line of master toymakers.

"How will the children know who the toys are from?" Nick asked.

"I'll spread the word. You just concentrate on the toys and the **LIST**," Sandy answered.

TAP!TAP!
TAP!TAP!

"What list?" Nick asked.

OFFICIAL

NAUGHTY	NICE ✓
Name	

"The official **NAUGHTY** and **NICE** List. You see, people tend to do better when there is a little incentive. They need a reason to do something. Children who are kind to others and obey their parents will earn the toys. We will need a list to keep track of all the nice children."

"How will I know?"

"Have **FAITH** - you'll know."

So Nick worked on the list, and Sandy got busy with her **LAUNCH** campaign—

which is a fancy way to say "**PLAN**."

She chose **RED** and **GREEN** as the colors they wanted to use for wrapping paper, decorations, and Nick's outfit. These are called "branding colors." She also asked some stores to tell people all about the toys, which they did—some even four months before Christmas Eve! This was generating so much excitement and encouraging all the children of the world to **BE KIND**!

There was a lot to do to be ready for Christmas, so on the days that Sandy was extra busy, Nick took care of the laundry and cooked dinner.

And when Nick had late nights in the toy shop with the elves, Sandy jumped in to take care of chores around the house. They stuck to their vows of always being equal partners.

Next, they needed to figure out how to get around the world in a vehicle that wouldn't pollute the atmosphere.

Luckily, the elves were friends with a local **REINDEER** farmer in the North Pole, so they hooked them up with eight great reindeer and a low-emissions **SLEIGH**.

They were all set with the reindeer and sleigh, but Nick had a big concern. "How will we possibly get to everyone's home to deliver my toys to all the children in the world in just one night?"

"**MAGIC**," Sandy said.

"We **BELIEVE** so strongly that every child in the whole world deserves a toy and that delivering toys will make the world a better place, and we know that you are the one who can do it."

"We believe it enough,

   and we've worked hard for it, so it simply is.

            IT'S MAGIC!"

The big day finally arrived –

CHRISTMAS EVE.

Sandy sent Nick on his way to deliver the toys, gave the elves the night off, and enjoyed a peppermint-infused bubble bath while sipping hot chocolate at home, alone, and it was wonderful.

THE MAGIC WORKED, AND THE TOYS WERE DELIVERED ALL AROUND THE WORLD!

Nick arrived home, and they celebrated with some milk and cookies, getting right back to work the next day to prepare for the next Christmas Eve. "I'm so proud of you, Mr. Claus," Sandy said. "Couldn't have done it without you, Mrs. Claus," Nick said.

When Sandy needed help, Nick stepped in, and when Nick needed support, she was there. They listened to each other, they always told the truth, and they loved each other more and more after each launch of Christmas Eve.

And every single year, they work together to make sure that children all around the world get a toy on Christmas.

The end.

Made in the USA
Middletown, DE
16 November 2019